# ALASKA ANIMAL BABIES

PHOTOGRAPHS BY **GAVRIEL JECAN** WRITTEN BY **DEB VANASSE**

**PAWS IV**

PUBLISHED BY SASQUATCH BOOKS

# Bald Eagle

With eyesight three times more powerful than ours, these young
eagles keep a close watch over the forest. More of these handsome birds
swoop and soar over Alaska than over the other forty-nine states combined.
They'll be easier to spot when they're four years old and have
grown white feathers on their heads and tails.

# Sea Otter

Want a ride? Sea otter pups like to travel on their mothers' chests, though they can float by themselves from birth. Otters blow bubbles into their own fur, adding extra air to keep warm in Alaska's chilly waters. When they fall asleep at sea, otters may grasp each other's paws in the same way that we hold hands.

# Dall Sheep

High on a mountaintop in Wrangell-St. Elias National Park, this lamb learned to walk within hours of birth. When she's older, she'll grow horns made of keratin. Your fingernails are made of keratin, too.

# Arctic Fox

When he was born, this arctic fox kit was so tiny you could have held him in the palm of your hand. His short legs and chubby body keep him warm on the treeless tundra. As the northern days grow short, his thick fur will turn as white as the drifting snow.

# Gray Wolf

Among gray wolves,
one parent stays with the
pups while the other hunts.
Wolves talk to each other
with howls and movements.
When a pup bumps his
mother's chin, he's telling
her he wants attention.
If you have a dog, it's
probably a descendant
of the wolf.

# Golden Plover

Can you find this golden plover chick? Her downy feathers blend perfectly with the plants and berries of the Arctic National Wildlife Refuge. She eats lots of tasty bugs so she can fatten up for a nonstop flight far across the ocean.

# Black-Tailed Deer

Think deer are quiet? Not black-tailed deer from Southeast Alaska. They baa, bleat, and grunt like sheep. And this fawn might get some funny looks if he joined your family for dinner. With no upper teeth, he has to gulp his food.

# Orca

Sometimes it's hard to stay still, especially if you're an orca whale calf. At naptime, the mothers rest by swimming close and slow. The babies would rather breach, slap, and dive, but they learn to wait for a whale in their pod to give the "wake-up call" before they start to play.

# Hawk Owl

Most owls cry *whoo, whoo*, but these northern hawk owls say *ki, ki, ki, ki, ki*. Hawk owls are born not in a nest, but in a hole in a tree. They hunt in daylight instead of at nighttime, and they're not afraid of people.

# Grizzly Bear

Grizzly bear cubs learn to fish from their mothers, but they'll eat more berries than fish—up to 200,000 berries a day when full grown. Grizzlies are very smart, and they hear and smell well, too. Cubs love to wrestle, swim, and climb scrubby willow trees.

# Red Fox

Red fox kits peer out from their den, curious but wary. Fox kits learn to hunt by stalking, springing, and pouncing on their prey. Their parents even let them fight among themselves to determine who's in charge.

# Merganser

They like to ride on their mother's back, but before long these baby mergansers will be diving for their dinner. Mergansers love to eat eels, fish, and mollusks. Their long bills have serrated edges like kitchen knives to help them catch their food.

# Musk Ox

This baby musk ox may look frightened, but if danger draws near, his herd will circle around to keep him safe. Long guard hairs and thick underfur protect musk oxen from bitter winter winds. Musk oxen rub against bushes and rocks, leaving clumps of fur that people gather to craft into soft, warm garments.

# Northern Fur Seal

Perched on one of the rocky Pribilof Islands, this northern fur seal uses his back flippers to run and climb. But once he grows up, he'll spend most of his time in the ocean. He'll even sleep there, bending into a circle so he can float with his nose above water.

# Polar Bear

Plodding over snow and ice, these polar bear cubs follow in their mother's tracks. They'll cover 1,500 miles by their first birthday. Along the way, they'll learn to hunt, using their keen noses to smell animals from far, far away.

# River Otter

This baby river otter learned to swim when she was eight weeks old. River otters love to splash, slide, wrestle, and play hide-and-seek. You might hear them hiss if they're angry or chirp if they think they're lost.

# Kittiwake

Like lots of neighbors? Kittiwake chicks share rocky cliffs in Southeast Alaska with millions of shorebirds. You can tell they're kittiwakes by their strange cries, which sound just like their name.

# Humpback Whale

Splash! A humpback whale calf makes a loud noise when he plays. His flippers flare like wings when he breaches, launching his huge body from the water. Humpback whales sing in haunting tones as they swim north. Once they reach Alaska, they quit singing and concentrate on eating—up to two tons of food a day.

# Sandhill Crane

Who's peering over the tundra grass? It's a sandhill crane chick, her neck stretched out like it will be when she learns to fly. Sandhill cranes are among the tallest and oldest bird species in the world. Yup'ik Eskimos call them "Sunday turkeys."

# Ptarmigan

These ptarmigan
are masters of masquerade.
In the summer, their
feathers blend perfectly
with rocks and brush. In
the winter, ptarmigan turn
almost pure white, growing
feathers on their legs and
feet to help them scurry
across the snow.

# Moose

This moose calf can swivel his ears like periscopes, listening for sounds of trouble. Should danger strike, his mother will come to the rescue. A mama moose will charge people, horses, cars, and even trains to defend her young.

# Emperor Goose

Eelgrass, anyone? How about some tasty sea lettuce or crowberries? Those are favorite foods of these emperor geese. Geese take good care of their chicks, fiercely defending them as they grow into some of the most beautiful water birds in Alaska.

# Trumpeter Swan

We're glad to see these trumpeter swan cygnets. Not so long ago, there were only seventy trumpeter swans left in the world. Now that we protect the Alaskan wetlands where swans are born, there are more than 16,000 of these magnificent birds.

# Mountain Goat

Huddling close, the mountain goat protects her baby from falling off slopes that are twice as steep as your stairs at home. With spreading hooves and strong front legs, these goats amble over the tall mountains of Glacier Bay National Park.

# Marmot

Who's whistling? The marmot's high-pitched warning call echoes over a mile. Marmots also hiss, yell, and bark. When danger nears, they flatten themselves against a rock. This young marmot will stay with his family in Denali National Park for two years before heading out on his own.

*With thanks to Dave Lorring and Tim Vanasse for sharing
their abundant knowledge of Alaskan wildlife.* — D. V.

Photographs ©2005 by Gavriel Jecan
Text ©2005 by Deb Vanasse

Printed in China
Published by Sasquatch Books
Distributed by Publishers Group West
12 11 10 09 08 07 06 05      6 5 4 3 2 1

Layout: Stewart A. Williams
Cover photo: Jeff Schultz/AlaskaStock

Jecan, Gavriel.
     Alaska animal babies / photographs by Gavriel Jecan ; written by Deb Vanasse.
p. cm.
ISBN 1-57061-433-4
1. Animals--Infancy--Alaska--Juvenile literature.   I. Vanasse, Deb. II. Title.

QL161.J43 2005
591.3´9´09798--dc22

2004059431


Sasquatch Books
119 South Main Street, Suite 400
Seattle, WA  98104
(206) 467-4300
www.sasquatchbooks.com
custserv@sasquatchbooks.com